Chuck's Unicorn Tinglers
Volume 1

CHUCK TINGLE

Love is real.

- Chuck Tingle

CONTENTS

ACKNOWLEDGMENTS

Thank you to my son, Jon Tingle. He teaches me to be a good man and has a really cool look.

No thank you, Ted Cobbler, who is disrespectful and keeps the whole block up with his loud music.

TAKEN BY THE GAY UNICORN BIKER

I don't believe in miracles; nor luck, nor magic. I don't believe in anything that I can't see with my own eyes or touch with my own skin, and it's been a long time since I have. Superstition is a plague.

Some people think that being skeptic is boring, but I'd like to think of myself as simply an appreciator of reality. I don't need to live in a fantasy world when real life is so full of brilliance and beauty.

Take, for example, this very moment.

I've been driving all night, desperately crossing the harsh Nevada desert towards Las Vegas for my brothers wedding. It's not to long of a drive from Los Angeles, clocking in at a little under five hours, but it can get grueling if you're forced to leave right after your shift ends at the gay bar where you work.

I managed to pull out of West Hollywood at two in the morning, and now the sun is coming up in front of me, bathing the glorious desert landscape with a beautiful wash of yellow and gold. It's absolutely stunning and completely real.

It's weird how much this firm grip on reality means to me, considering the fact that my parents and brother are so religious. But, in a lot of ways, I think that's probably the reason I turned out the way that I did. It's not easy growing up in a Christian household as a flamboyantly gay child, and although they all still claim to love me after I came out of the closet, it's clear they like my brother, Jared, just the slightest bit more.

This is why I can't be late to the wedding, and why I can't stop glancing at the clock on my dashboard as the minutes count endlessly upward. I need to prove that I'm not a complete mess out in Los Angeles on my own, that I've got my shit together.

I'm driving as fast as I can, but by now I'm also too tired to focus and the whole thing really just starts to make me uncomfortable. Speed and sleep rarely mix, and right now I'm flirting with disaster. Still, I've gotta get there somehow.

"You'll make it." I say aloud to myself, looking off into the sunrise and trying to focus on the natural beauty before me. This is reality, right here and now. I might be late and my parents and brother will certainly look down on me for it, but the sun will still rise and the sun will still set.

I take a deep breath, in and out, trying desperately not to stress.

If it isn't already clear, I'm a recovering anger junkie. These days you'd never even know what it used to be like, the way I would change into a complete asshole at the flip of a switch. It's destroyed every relationship that I've ever had, but these days I'm feeling better about it. I think that I might just be ready to find something meaningful again, maybe even love.

I've started to look inward, and it's working.

I take another deep breath, holding it longer this time before exhaling as the car roars down the long stretch of highway.

"You're going to make it to your brothers wedding." I say to myself again. "Stay positive, Mario."

For the briefest of moments I close my eyes, trying hard to mediate just a split second and somehow recharge my batteries. Showing up to the wedding is the easy part, after all, but showing up bright eyed and busy tailed was going to be difficult. I've only got two hours to spare.

Suddenly, the car lurches as I dip down off of the side of the road. My eyes by open and I swerve wildly, my hands gripping tightly onto the steering wheel as I try desperately to self-correct. I'm simply going way too fast.

The next thing I know, one of the tires has hit a massive triangular rock and my car is being launched into the air, flipped one entire rotation as I scream bloody murder and hold on for dear life.

Fortunately, I'm wearing my seatbelt, and I remain inside the car as it barrel rolls across the road without being tossed out through the glass windshield.

I'm fine, but the car itself is not so lucky. There is a loud snap as the vehicle lands and the axel breaks in half, dropping the car onto the pavement below and immediately ripping the two front wheels to shreds.

I skid to a stop amid a cloud of dust and debris, terribly shaken up but otherwise okay. Steam rises up from under the hood of the vehicle and drifts away and I struggle to unbuckle my seatbelt. I climb out from the drivers seat, staggering into the light of the rising Neveda sun.

"Fuck!" I exclaim aloud, immediately recognizing that my car may or may not be totaled. Searing anger boils within me, but I remember to focus and somehow cool myself down into a quiet simmer. "Just chill." I tell myself. "Just chill out, it's going to be okay."

I quickly realize that my insurance will cover this, even though it's entirely my fault, and at the end of the day I'm not going to take much of a hit financially. Besides, the gay bar that I work as is incredibly high end, and the tips that I make alone are double some folks salary. In other words, I'll be fine.

The real problem, however, is that I'm only a few short hours away from proving to my family, once and for all, that I'm not a complete fuck up. The car situation is not exactly helping my cause.

I let my gaze linger over the wreckage, reeling from the intense physical trauma that still lingers within my body. My nerves are at full alert and my neck is killing me.

I look up and down the road, trying to see if I can spot any other rides headed my way, but there is absolutely nothing but wide open desert. Trying to make good time, I took my best attempt at finding an alternate route and somehow ended up on these back roads along the way. It's great for avoiding traffic, but I could sure use a lift right about now and who knows when the next one is coming.

With nothing left to do, I just start walking.

It's early enough in the morning that the desert heat hasn't yet started to beat down too harshly but, with every step I take, the temperature seems to grow warmer and warmer.

By the time the car has disappeared behind me I'm drenched with sweat, yearning for someone, anyone, to come driving by and save me with a generous ride, even if it's just to the nearest gas station.

I've almost entirely given up hope when suddenly I notice a shiny silver object rising up over the hill behind me. It's almost too far away to see, like a tiny glinting spec on the horizon line, but from where I stand I can hear it barreling over the asphalt. It's a motorcycle.

Immediately I stop walking and begin to wave for the riders attention, hopping up and down as I throw my arms wildly in the air on the side of the road. I'd been so busy hoping that someone would drive by that I never even considered the fact that they probably won't stop for me, but I've got to try.

Fortunately though, as the vehicle draws closer it begins to slow until, eventually, the motorcycle pulls up next to me and stops completely. It's only then that I realize the rider is a beautiful, white unicorn, with a long flowing main and a glorious pearly horn jutting out from the top of his head. The unicorn turns to me and nods in acknowledgement.

"Where are you headed?" The biker unicorn asks in a gruff voice.

"Vegas." I tell him, to desperate to be bothered by the fact that my savior is not human.

"Guess it's your lucky day." The unicorn says, his tail whipping back and forth in the air as it hangs over the back seat of the bike. "I'm headed there, too. Unless that's your car back there, in which case it's probably not your lucky day."

I shake my head. "Nope. I don't know what happened but the thing it totaled."

"I'd say you're probably right about that." The unicorn says, stopping the asphalt a bit with its hoof. "Well, let's hit the road, huh? Climb on behind me."

I do as I'm told, deciding it's best not to tell this majestic creature that I don't believe in luck as I walk over to the large motorcycle. I swing my leg around the back, then scoot up against the unicorn.

"What's your name?" I ask. "I'm Mario."

"Kirk." The unicorn tells me, then neighs loudly as we take off down the road, the bike rumbling powerfully between my legs.

The next thing I know, we're back on track, flying towards Vegas at full speed and without a minute to spare. I wrap my arms around Kirk and hold on tight, noticing the pleasant warmth of his body against mine. I had never seen a unicorn before in real life, and I find myself surprised by how masculine his beauty is. Besides the slight pink shimmer of the creature's mane and horn, there is nothing girly about this muscular beast. In fact, this particular unicorn is actually looking pretty badass in his leather jacket, jeans and boots.

"You seem tense." I shout into the unicorn's ear over the loud rumbling of the motor beneath us. "Why are you headed to Vegas?"

Kirk pauses for a moment before answering, choosing his words wisely. "I'm not so much heading *to* Vegas. More like heading *away* from California."

"Oh shit." I offer. "What happened?"

"Bad breakup." The unicorn tells me. "Really bad."

We sit in silence for a moment, letting the sound of the wind rushing past fill our ears.

"Well, I don't really know you all that well." I offer. "But it sounds like she lost out on a pretty good unicorn."

"He." The unicorn corrects me. "*He* lost out on a good guy."

"You're gay?" I ask, surprised. "Me too!"

"No shit?" Says the unicorn with a laugh. "I'm normally so good with that, I can always tell."

"Not this time." I smile. "I get that a lot though, my ex used to tell me that I acted too straight."

The unicorn nods, staring out across the road ahead of us. "Sounds like both of us have asshole ex guys."

I pull tighter against the unicorn, feeling the beat of his massive heart against my body. He's an incredible creature, so perfectly toned and strong. I have never before been attracted to anything other than a human male, but being here on this bike with Kirk has, admittedly, opened my eyes to a different kind of beauty. I can't help but feel a strange twinge of arousal deep within me, and I'm just barely able to keep myself from growing and erection right here against the unicorn's back.

"So why are *you* going to Vegas?" The unicorn questions. "I wasn't going to ask, but now that we're getting to know each other so well I figured you might as well tell me."

"Nothing too exciting." I say. "My brothers wedding."

"That sounds really exciting!" The unicorn protests. "It's your brother!"

"We're not exactly close." I explain.

Whenever I tell people about the fact that my brother and me don't get along, people always respond with the same thing. 'He's your brother, you'll figure it out.' Kirk, on the other hand, has nothing to say other than, "I'm sorry to hear that."

It's not a dismissive version of the phrase, nor an empty one; for once

I feel a sincere empathy for my feelings on the matter. Kirk isn't trying to change me, he just wants to listen, and that alone is much more than any man as ever really offered.

"You're pretty cool, you know that?" I say to the unicorn.

Kirk cracks a smile and nods to himself. "I suppose I'm alright."

His casual unicorn demeanor is so incredible to me, and suddenly, despite my best efforts, I find myself getting turned on.

"Whoa." Kirk says with a laugh, sensing the hardening of my cock up against his back. "You getting excited back there, buddy?"

"No." I protest, defensively.

"It sure doesn't feel like it." The unicorn prods with a laugh. "That feels like a big fucking human cock pressed up against my back."

I don't say a word, completely embarrassed.

"You ever fucked a unicorn?" Kirk asks me suddenly.

I can immediately sense a change in his tone, a new direction in his unicorn mannerisms all the way down to the way the he turns his large beastly head to speak to me.

"No, I can't say that I have." I explain. "You're the first one I've met."

Kirk nods. "Yep, there's not a lot of us out there, not a lot of gay one's either."

"I didn't even realize you existed." I confess.

Kirk scoffs. "Come on now, that's just rude."

"I'm sorry, I'm sorry." I offer. "Anyway…"

The word drifts off behind us as we continue down the road, the tension between me and Kirk the unicorn biker growing to incredible heights. There is something comforting about just being here with him, as if I've suddenly been blessed with the assurance that everything will work out in the end. He's a protector, a figure of power that radiates with support, companionship, and gay lust. My body aches for him.

I find myself running my fingers through the unicorn's shimmering mane, unable to stop my roving hands. "Do you believe in love at first sight?" I ask Kirk.

"I don't know." He tells me, "Why?"

I hesitate, not wanting to just lay all my cards out there on the table, but then I take the plunge. "I feel something between us. I don't believe in miracles or anything like that, and I know it sounds crazy but I think that I love you... I think that I *want* you. Right now."

"Right now?" Kirk confirms, slowing down the motorcycle. "Don't you have somewhere to be?"

"I don't give a fuck." I tell him.

Almost immediately, Kirk pulls over onto the side of the road and climbs off of the motorcycle. I step off with him, and then moments later we are meeting under the desert sun next to a giant, flat boulder. Kirk and me embrace each other feverishly, our lips locked in a passionate kiss.

My heart rate elevated, my body trembling, I'm happy to finally release all of the powerful tension that has been building up inside of me. I'm trembling with desire, wanting nothing more than to take his massive, gay unicorn biker cock inside of my body. I want to pleasure him, to make him understand the way that he makes me ache.

Without another set of eyes for miles on this empty stretch of desert highway, I quickly tear off my shirt and watch gladly as Kirk does the same. His body is utterly incredible, perfect and muscular in its majestic, beastly form. I touch him gently with my hands and then work my way down the unicorn's toned, muscular chest.

Suddenly overwhelmed with passion, I drop to my knees and unbutton Kirk's pants, pulling them down and letting his massive unicorn cock spring forth.

"Holy shit." I gasp. "Your dick is fucking enormous!"

The confident unicorn biker gives me a wink. "Think you can handle it?"

Instead of answering I decide to show him, opening wide and swallowing Kirk's shaft deep into my hungry mouth. The gorgeous beast lets out a satisfied neigh, leaning back and lifting his head skyward like a howling wolf of the desert.

I move up and down, letting Kirk's rod slip gracefully between my lips as I pleasure him. With one hand I cradle his hanging balls, and with the other I reach up and take his hoof in mine, grasping tightly.

"You're incredible." Kirk moans.

I push down farther and farther until hitting the edge of my gag reflex, which causes me to stop abruptly. Kirk's size is just too much to take, and I struggle against his rod, retching as I push the limits of my body. I simply can't take his size. Instead, I find myself stuck, and eventually I'm forced to come up for air in a frantic gasp.

"Are you alright?" Kirk asks.

"Yes." I assure him. "I just need to do this, let me try."

"You don't need to do anything." He tells me. "You don't need to impress me."

I shake my head. "I need to do this, Kirk."

I center myself and then try again, this time relaxing my throat as much as possible as Kirk's unicorn cock slides deeper and deeper into me. His length is incredible, and at first I retch a little as it hits the back of my throat. Moments later, however, I somehow manage to relax enough that Kirk's massive dick slides all the way inside. I proudly look up at him and give a playful wink, Kirk's shaft entirely consumed as my lips press lightly up against his rock hard unicorn abs.

"Fuck." Is all that this amazing man can manage to get out, overwhelmed by my expert deep throating skills. "That's incredible, Mario."

The sound of my own name sends a pleasant chill down my spine. This is all that I had ever wanted. To find love when I least expected it, out here in the desert in a time of need. I was stranded and alone, fighting for my life against the heat and the natural elements and then suddenly, with the help of one gay biker unicorn, everything changed. Maybe miracles do happen, I think to myself, maybe I was wrong all along.

Moments later, I find Kirk carefully pulling me up to my feet with his powerful unicorn teeth. He kisses me deeply and then pushes me back against the flat rock next to us, where I lay happily as the beautiful beast removes my jeans and tosses them to the side. My briefs come off next, and suddenly I find myself completely exposed to the warm desert air.

Kirk leans down and immediately gets to work licking my hard cock, which sends all kinds of incredible volts of pleasure throughout my body. I arch my back against the warm stone as Kirk satisfies my senses, my hands finding their way around to the back of his head and pulling him even tighter against me.

The creature certainly knows how to use his tongue, finding no trouble at all with quickly bringing my body dangerously close to orgasm.

Eventually, Kirk starts to suck me off, taking my entire shaft easily into his large unicorn mouth. He pumps his head up and down on my length, pleasuring me skillfully between his majestic lips. I let out a long, satisfied moan, which seems to kick him into overdrive, pumping his head faster and faster over my length.

I'm going to cum soon. The feeling builds within me in wave after blissful wave, every one of them becoming more powerful than the last until finally I just can't take it anymore and I force myself to push him back.

"I want to cum." I tell the unicorn. "But I want to do it with you inside of me."

Kirk smiles and pulls me down the boulder slightly so that my muscular gay ass is hanging right off of the edge. Next, he aligns his rock hard shaft with my puckered butthole, his head teasing against my entrance while I beg for him to push it in.

Kirk is much larger than any of the human cocks that I've ever taken anally, and I have to admit that I'm slightly fearful of what his incredible size could do to my body, but I try my best to play it off and be fearless. Still, the anxiety is there, but thanks to the loving nature of my new unicorn lover, it becomes exciting and erotic, only adding to our playful and lusty encounter. I feel safe around Kirk, free to be myself even if that means getting a little nervous.

I collect my wits, then reach down and spread my gay ass open for him.

"Fuck me!" I demand. "Fuck me with your giant unicorn cock!"

Kirk stops for a moment. "I want you to beg for it."

"Fuck." I start, reaching down and grabbing a hold of his large beastly body with one hand. "Me." As I finish repeating the phrase, I pull Kirk forward and his mammoth cock disappears completely inside of my asshole, stretching my tightness to the brink.

I let out a loud groan, not entirely prepared to take his substantial size within my butt.

As I look up at the beautiful sky above us, clouds drifting calmly across the open blue, I can't think of any better moment to open my heart up than this. It's everything I ever dreamed it could be, me and my unicorn lover locked in a passionate embrace that defies species or sexualities.

Kirk begins to pump in and out of my butt, slowly but firmly as I tremble from his skilled touch. My legs are spread wide for him, held back as he slams into me at an ever-escalating speed. Soon enough, Kirk is hammering into me with everything he's got, his hips pounding loudly against the side of the boulder.

Once again, I can feel the profound sensation of an impending prostate orgasm blossoming deep within. It grows quickly, spreading out across my body in a series of violent quakes until my entire being is convulsing. There is too much pleasure locked up inside, bubbling over without any place left to go.

I reach down and start to frantically beat off my own rock hard cock, rapidly pumping my hand over it's length in time with the pounding of Kirk's powerful thrusts.

"Oh my god." I start to mumble. "Oh my god."

"I love you so much." Kirk the unicorn tells me, his eyes aflame with truth and passion. "I want to be your biker unicorn lover forever!"

"I love you, too!" I tell him, my legs suddenly kicking out straight. "I'm cumming!"

Kirk doesn't let up for a second as the prostate orgasm surges through me like a lightning bolt, pounding away at my muscular frame with his massive unicorn body. All of the tension from the last few hours is suddenly released within me, exploding across every ounce of my being with blinding love. Hot ropes of jizz explode from the end of my shaft, blasting out into the air and splattering everywhere.

I let out a blood-curdling howl of pleasure that echos out across the desert landscape, cascading across the hills and valleys until it bounces back to us. I'm outside of my body now, looking down at myself as I writhe and spasm on the edge this flat desert boulder. Tears of joy are flowing down my cheeks in beautiful glistening streaks, truly happy within my own skin.

I suddenly realize that Kirk is cumming as well, buckling forward as he ejects several pumps of semen within my asshole. His eyes are clenched tight as he lets out a guttural neigh of his own, throwing his head back and shutting his eyes in an expression of pure satisfaction.

The entire experience seems to defy time and space, stretching on and on for what feels like forever until suddenly I'm thrown back into reality, lying in exhaustion with Kirk's large unicorn body on top of me, breathing heavy.

"That was amazing." I whisper into his ear.

"No, you're amazing." He tells me.

"There's something I want you to do for me." I tell him. "Something important."

The biker unicorn nods. "Anything."

"Come to my brother's wedding with me."

The wedding goes beautifully, and is surprisingly classy for it's tongue-in-cheek Las Vegas setting. I had expected a drive through chapel with an Elvis impersonator overseeing the ceremony, but instead I was greeted by a beautiful venue in one of the nicest hotels on the strip.

My entire family was there, and when I pushed through the doors to greet them with plenty of time to spare, their eyes lit up in surprise. Showing up on time to the wedding shouldn't mean that much, but for me even being here at all went a huge way in showing that, even though I was gay, I didn't have to be the black sheep of the family.

Not only that, but everyone loved Kirk. At first I was worried that they'd have a problem with the fact that he rode motorcycles and came off as a bit of a rough and tumble guy, but he cleans up nice. Nobody at the wedding had ever seen a unicorn before, either, and Kirk was nice enough to answer questions and provide rides around the room during the reception.

I watch from afar as my father hoots and hollers, riding my new boyfriend around the banquet hall as the rest of the wedding party looks on in amazement. My newlywed brother is standing next to me and he puts his hand on my shoulders.

"You seem... really good." My brother, Jared, says. "Chilled out or something."

I laugh. "I think that I am."

"Thanks so much for being here." Jared tells me. "It means a lot."

"Don't mention it." I say, winking at Kirk as he passes by. "I wouldn't miss it for the world."

MY ASS IS HAUNTED BY THE GAY UNICORN COLONEL

As I approach the old plantation house, my body fills with a strange sensation. It's a feeling that is not entirely new to me, but it is also one strictly reserved for occasions of extreme tension and caution. To call this emotion fear is flat-out incorrect, it is not fear but something even deeper and more subliminal. This feeling is the remnant of a long forgotten instinct, one that taps deep into my mind and then connects itself to some other world, some other plane of existence.

And then, just like that, the feeling disappears.

A chill runs down my spine as I look up at the windows of the old mansion, framed perfectly between two large weeping willows here in the deep forest of northern Georgia.

For a moment, I catch a glimpse of someone standing in the window of a second story bedroom, a unicorn with a long white mane and a large, pearly white horn. The majestic beast moves out of the way as soon as I see him, letting the curtain fall back into place.

"Hello there!" The voice on an elderly woman suddenly calls from the front porch. "Welcome to Blue Bayou Bed and Breakfast!"

I smile and wave as my gaze falls upon a small old lady in her casual summer wear, hurrying down the steps to greet me. When I booked my room I had no idea I would be receiving such a warm welcome, and it's a pleasant relief from the usual indifference that I get from places like this.

Get in, pay us, get out, is usually the motto, especially when the ghost sightings have reached a level of notoriety that turns an establishment into less of a bed and breakfast, and more of a tourist trap.

"You must be Roger." The old woman says, taking one of my bags. "I'm Melody. It's nice to meet you, come along right this way."

It all happens to fast that I barely have time to protest. "Oh come on now, I'll carry my bags up!" I tell her, legitimately worried that she's about to break a bone simply hoisting up my leather weekender.

"Don't be silly!" Melody creaks in her own cheerful way. "You're my guest, I so rarely get guests anymore."

I sigh and follow her up the front porch and into the house. "I thought people were coming from all over the world to catch a glimpse of Colonel Peach's ghost, shouldn't that be bringing in some business?"

"Oh, it did for a while." Melody tells me, placing my bag in the entryway and then leading me into the dining room. "But it seems like people aren't interested in history like they used to be. Nobody cares about an old civil war spirit I guess"

As I round the corner of the dining room I'm immediately hit with the pleasant aroma of savory, delicious food. There are two places set at the end of the table, one for Melody and one for me, and an entire assortment of roast vegetables, grilled meats, and a cauldron of soup in the middle.

"Oh my god." I gasp in astonishment. "You can't be serious, this looks incredible."

"Well, I figured you probably had a long journey today so I figured I'd whip up some dinner." Melody explains. "It's just the two of us tonight but I reckoned that if I'm gonna go through the trouble of cooking, I might as well do it right."

Melody sits down in her chair and I follow suit, smiling graciously as she dishes up some of the creamy soup into a bowl and hands it to me. Even if I don't see any colonial ghosts on this trip, this is still one hell of a bed and breakfast.

"Can I ask?" I start. "If it's just the two of us here, then who was that unicorn upstairs when I drove in?"

"Upstairs?" Melody asks, slightly confused.

"Yeah, he was staring down at me from the far left window." I explain.

Melody freezes as she hears this, a smile slowly creeping across her wrinkled old face. "A unicorn, you say?"

I nod, not quite seeing what the big deal is at this point.

Melody sits in silence for just a moment longer and then stands up. "Dinner can wait for just a moment, I think you'll want to see this." The elderly woman leaves the dining room and heads back across the hall to what appears to be the main living quarters; two sofas, a fireplace, a mantle, and hanging above it a massive oil painting.

I follow Melody, but the second that I lay my eyes upon the strange portrait I stop, gazing up in wonder at the incredible sight that suspends before more. There in the thick strokes of vivid color sits a familiar face, one that I recognize almost immediately. It's the unicorn that I spotted in the window upstairs.

The creature looks absolutely regal, sitting atop a horse with the wind blowing through his sparkling unicorn mane. He's wearing a dark uniform and carrying a flag that waves in the wind behind him.

"Is that the unicorn that you saw in the window?" Melody asks.

I nod.

"That's Colonel Peach, he's been dead since the civil war." The old woman informs me.

This information is almost too shocking to comprehend, a revelation so strange that I have to silently repeat it back to myself over and over again until finally it clicks. I had just seen the ghost with my very own eyes.

Melody is kind enough to let me stay in the Colonel's old chambers tonight, which is precisely the room that I saw his single-horned ghost just hours earlier. The room is slightly chilly but beautifully arranged, featuring heavy oak furniture that has probably been here since the manor was built all those years ago.

The room itself gives me that same spooky feeling that I got upon arrival at these haunted grounds, an eerie kind of presence that seems to be lurking within each and every shadow.

As it grows later, the silver moonlight begins to stretch longer into the room. I'm lying in bed, reading quietly over some recently published papers on the paranormal.

Suddenly, I jump, a loud knock against the hardwood floors drawing my attention to the closed bedroom door before me.

"Hello?" I call out. "Miss Melody?"

This particular room has not yet been retrofitted for modern electricity, so I have been reading by candlelight. I glance over as the tiny flame flickers and struggles to stay alive, fighting against some strange cold wind as it gusts through the room with supernatural speed.

There is no response to my inquisitive call, but as I listen closely I can faintly hear what appears to be the wild cries of a civil war battle, the sounds echoing within my ears. I can hear the clap of muskets firing and the shouting of battle commands. A bungle rings out over the sound of thundering hooves as soldiers ride into battle. It's an utterly frightening illusion in its stark realness, and can only be perceived as false because it simply makes no sense.

My heart pounding within my chest, I watch as the doorknob to my bedroom begins to turn slowly. There is a loud metallic click and then moments later the door itself starts to open as a dark figure emerges.

"You called?" Comes the voice of Melody.

I let out a massive sigh of both relief and, of course, disappointment. I'm here to see a ghost, after all.

"Did you…" I stammer. "Did you hear that?"

"Hear what?" Melody asks.

"All of that fighting? Those war sounds?" I continue.

Melody just shakes her head. "No, I'm afraid that I didn't, but it sounds like being in this room has spooked you quite a bit. Are you sure you don't want me to put you up somewhere else?"

"Oh no." I tell the caring elderly woman. "I'm here to see the colonel, and this seems like the best place to do it."

Melody turns to leave and then stops for a moment, hesitating. She turns back around. "Roger, why is it that you are so interested in seeing these spirits for yourself."

I take a deep breath, closing my book and setting it down on the bedside table next to me. "Long ago, when I was just a nineteen-year-old fresh out of school, I took a trip to Spain. It was incredible, the food, the men." I tell her, letting Melody in on a subtle hint about my sexuality, in case she didn't already notice. "Anyway, I was there for a month and during that time I met a beautiful white unicorn named Paulo. He was so handsome, and so good to me. I rode around the city on his back all day and, in the evenings, Paulo would take me back to his flat and we would make love."

Melody gets a faint little twinkle in her eye. "Awe, that sounds very sweet."

I nod. "It was, it was. Back in those days unicorn and human relationships were looked down upon, but we didn't care. When Paulo and me were together it was like we could take on anything, change the world. I don't know if you believe in soul mates, Miss Melody, but I can assure you they are real."

"I believe." Melody says, smiling to herself.

"Then I'm guessing you know what it's like to loose your soul mate as well." I say, tearing up a bit. "You see, Paulo the unicorn was hoof hearted, meaning his heart was the size of a hoof, much too small for a unicorn of his size. I didn't know at the time, but he only had a few weeks left to live."

As I say this Melody places her hand over her heart, hurting for me as I remember my long lost lover.

"After, Paulo passed away." I continue. "I've been obsessed with the afterlife. I just want to know if he's still out there somewhere, my handsome Spanish unicorn."

"I'm sure he's out there." Melody assures me. "Looking down on you."

We stand in silence for a moment, before Melody nods and backs out into the hallway. She closes the door quietly behind her.

I grab my book off of the bedside table and start to read again.

I only make it a few sentences in before the words start to blur together in a meaningless mess. Getting emotional about Paulo my unicorn lover has made me tired, and before I know it I find myself drifting off to sleep.

I'm not sure how long I've been out when I awaken, but I sit up abruptly and suck in a huge gasp of air. My book, which had been resting on my lap, falls to the floor next to the bed with a light thump as I attempt to figure out exactly what it was that startled me awake so abruptly.

Faintly, I can hear my own name drifting through the night air. It sounds as though it's coming from right outside my window, emanating from somewhere in the front yard of this spooky old manor.

Cautiously, I climb to my feet and tiptoe over to the window, looking out onto the moon soaked lawn.

My breath catches in my throat. There before me, in all of his majestic unicorn ghost glory, is Colonel Peach. The unicorn colonel sits atop his powerful steed in full uniform, looking up at me as I gaze down at him. He's just as handsome as the painting that hangs downstairs, and despite my best efforts I almost immediately find myself just as aroused as I am afraid.

The sound of my own name still echoes through the trees. "Roger, roger." It's as if the unicorn colonel is begging me to run down to him and let him pick me up in his big, strong, ghost arms.

Compelled by some supernatural force, I turn away from the window, ready to sprint down to the colonel and give myself to him, but he's already here with me. I stop abruptly, shocked as I discover that the ghost has somehow instantly appeared within my room, no more than five feet away.

Now that I'm this close I can see that the colonel's body is slightly transparent, shimmering faintly as it sparkles with a strange unicorn magic. I can also see now how incredibly handsome this beast is, from his pearly horn to his heavy hooves, which poke out from the pants of his beautiful civil war uniform.

"Roger." The unicorn colonel says. "I have come here to deliver a message from beyond. I have come to bring you a message from Paulo."

The sound of my dead lovers name causes my heart to skip a beat. "What is it?" I stammer. "Tell me."

As I say the words I can feel a slight tingling begin deep within my ass, in a place that only Paulo could reach with his massive unicorn cock. In this moment I realize that Paulo's spirit is inside of me, haunting my ass.

"Paulo has a message from the great beyond." The unicorn colonel tells me. "A message of passion and fire, a message of love."

"I can feel it." I admit. "I can feel him deep within my butt."

The unicorn colonel nods. "Yes, but he's always been there, haunting your ass while you worked, slept… cried."

"He was there all along." I repeat.

The unicorn colonel nods. "Even though he's not powerful enough yet to manifest himself in physical form, he wanted me to pleasure you the way that he cannot."

At first I'm not exactly sure what Colonel Peach is saying, the strange invitation bouncing off of my brain a few times before finally sinking in. When I realize what he's getting at, however, I can't help being overwhelmed with a powerful arousal that immediately floods into my veins.

"You mean, Paulo want's us to fuck?" I ask, my voice trembling.

"He want's to give you pleasure." Says the Colonel Peach. "And right now this is the best way for him to do that."

I close my eyes and try to grapple with the idea of giving myself to a lover other than Paulo. Since Paulo's death, I hadn't slept with a single soul, unicorn or otherwise, and the idea alone seemed daunting. Still, just the suggestion had gotten my so worked up, my dick rock hard within my boxer briefs and just begging to be unleashed. Besides, this is what Paulo wants for me.

I swallow hard and then step forward so that I'm just inches away from the ghostly unicorn. "I want you." I say, letting my hand drift lower and lower until it reaches Colonel Peach's belt buckle, which I unclasp.

"I want you, too." The handsome dead unicorn says, finally giving in.

I undo his belt and then slowly unzip the Colonel's pants, which reveal no civil war era underwear underneath.

Instead, I'm greeted by this sight of his beautiful throbbing member, which springs forth from the fabric as soon as I let it. Colonel Peach is hard as a rock and aching to be touched, his enormous unicorn cock jutting fiercely out towards me.

I smile and slowly drop down into a squat before the beast, so that his shaft is pointed directly at my chiseled face, and then look up at him with my soulful gay eyes.

"Do you want me to suck you off?" I ask playfully. "For Paulo?"

The unicorn colonel doesn't answer, silent for a moment as he takes me in with his eerie, ghostly presence. He seems just as fascinated by me as I am of him.

"I said, do you want me to suck off that big, fat, unicorn cock of yours?" I repeat.

Finally, Colonel Peach breaks his silence; the single word barely making it out of his gently parted lips alive. "Yes."

With that, I open wide and engulf Colonel Peach's cock with my mouth, pushing my head down along the length of his shaft until I reach the edge of my gag reflex. I close my eyes and focus, relaxing my body until finally I feel comfortable going even deeper. Eventually, I reach the base of his shaft with my lips, my face pushed right up against Colonel Peach's hard unicorn abs as he fills my throat entirely.

The creature lets out a long, satisfied moan, his entire body shaking from my masterful deep throat. I can feel the colonel's hoof hands press gently on the back of my head and hold me there, hesitating, as if he's still not entirely sure that he wants to commit to this favor for a ghostly friend.

But the ship has already sailed, and as I reach up and begin to play with the beast's hanging balls that rest against my chin, the feeling is just too much for Colonel Peach to ignore. He starts to pump me up and down his shaft, slowly at first and then gaining speed as the waves of pleasure start to overwhelm him.

I look up at the colonel and we lock eyes, his cock planted firmly in my throat. I can't help but give him a playful little wink, and suddenly he's over the edge completely, a crazed look of sexual passion overwhelming his expression as he rocks his hips against me.

I slowly pull his unicorn pants father and farther down until he's able to step out of them. Releasing Colonel Peach from my mouth I stand up and give him a deep kiss.

"Lie down on the bed." I instruct.

The unicorn ghost starts to protest slightly but I'm firm with my instructions. I grab his hoof in my hand and then force it down the front of my boxer briefs, letting him feel the hard thickness of my massive rod.

"Do you want this dick?" I ask plainly.

"I can't." The colonel explains. "I'm a unicorn, I'll break it."

"Me and Paulo used to fuck on our bed all the time." I tell him. "So that's what we're gonna do."

The unicorn understands, and moments later he removes his uniform completely and climbs up into the massive oak bed, which creaks under the weight of his massive unicorn body.

"You look good." I coo, egging the beast on.

Finding his confidence, Colonel Peach sprawled out on his bed before me, his cock hard and standing at full attention. It's much longer and thicker than I had even realized when it was engulfed within my mouth, and now that I can fully inspect the translucent, ghostly shaft's incredible size I'm even more impressed.

I slowly strut across the hardwood floors towards Colonel Peach, enjoying the way that his eyes flicker and dance across my ripped, muscular body. At this point, he can't help but stare.

Seductively, I climb up onto the bed and crawl towards him, popping my gay ass out into the air as I go and then eventually positioning myself directly over his huge body. I take Colonel Peach's hooves and pull them above his head, controlling him completely as I make my way down his ripped chest and abs with a series of sensual kisses.

Despite my newfound confidence, however, I find myself trembling with anticipation and fear. I know that it's Paulo who want's this, but I can't keep myself from imaging my lover watching over us, analyzing every move that we make. Moments later, however, I feel that familiar tingle deep within my ass; a reminder.

I close my eyes and take a deep breath, and then let go of any reservations I had left within me. Immediately, I reach down and take Colonel Peach's huge rod into my hand, aligning him with the puckered tightness of my gay asshole.

"Oh fuck." The colonel groans instinctively as I push down onto him, letting out a soft moan of my own as the powerful beast slides up inside of me, my asshole expanding to it's limits in an effort to take his brutal insertion.

His presence fills me with a sensation that is familiar and warm, a distant memory that had been locked away until this very moment. I bite my lip instinctively and start to grind against him with firm, deep swoops of my hips.

I'm not fully prepared for the long forgotten sensation of being entered by a unicorn lover, and almost immediately I'm beside myself with pleasure, my body trembling and quaking as I ride him. It's as if all the sexual bliss that I've been staving myself from has been here the whole time, hiding away in some dark corner of my being and just waiting to be released by the right gay beast.

"Oh my god." I pant loudly, repeating the words over and over again. "Oh my god, oh my god."

Colonel Peach's hooves are on my hips, helping to pull me up and down across him in an incredible pulsing rhythm. I can feel all of his powerful strength though this minor touch; he's showing restraint, his body handling me firmly but with care.

"Let go." I tell him. "Just pound me like my dead unicorn lover would."

That does the trick. Suddenly, Colonel Peach is sitting up and flipping me over with his muscular unicorn legs, turning me around to that I'm facing away from him on my hands and knees. I look back at him and smile.

There's a loud crack as Colonel Peach slaps my ass with a hoof, hard, then he grabs me by my hips and pulls me back towards him with ease. He takes his cock and maneuvers it into the entrance of my anal tightness. There's a fire in Colonel Peach's eyes as he thrusts into me, the massive rod filling my butthole entirely as I cry out with a yelp of pleasure. Colonel Peach wastes no time now, immediately getting to work as he rams my body from behind.

I grip tightly onto the bed sheets in front of me, bracing myself against the unicorn colonel's powerful slams. There is an animalistic nature to his thrusting now, more brazen than sensual, but the ghostly creature still knows exactly how to hit my prostate on the inside. Somehow, this is even more of a turn on than before, his gentlemanly demeanor finally cracking before my very eyes, the poker face slipping away and finally revealing the sexual beast underneath.

"Harder!" I scream back at him, never more turned on my entire life. "Fuck me harder like the little human twink that I am!"

Colonel Peach doesn't need to be told twice, picking up speed until he is absolutely pummeling me with everything that he's got, slamming my asshole from behind with gay reckless abandon.

I reach down and grab a hold of my cock, beating myself off furiously.

Deep within my stomach I can now feel the first beautiful sparks of orgasm begin to fly, lighting a tiny fire that slowly but surely begins to creep its way out across my body. I can't help but start to tremble and quake as the sensation consumes me, filling me with a strange warmth from head to toe.

The tremors of pleasant sensation keep coming in awesome waves, the space between them drawing shorter until finally it just becomes one giant ball of pleasure that envelops my body. I clench my teeth tightly and let out a long hiss, frantically grasping at the last straws of reality before a powerful orgasm pushes me over the edge.

I'm outside myself now, looking down at my body as I cum harder than I ever have. Jizz erupts from the head of my cock, splattering onto the bed sheets before me in a beautiful pattern of milky white. It's a satisfaction that can barely be described, a blinding fullness that consumes me perfectly. I throw my head back and let out a howl of ecstasy, unable to contain all of this sensation within. In this moment, I know that Paulo is with me, haunting my ass with Colonel Peach.

I don't have long to mull on this, however, because seconds later the colonel is shaking as well, his massive unicorn body preparing for an orgasm of his own.

"Cum all over me!" I demand fiercely. "Shoot that load all over this handsome gay face of mine!"

Colonel Peach pulls out and gives his cock three final pumps with his hand, then grips tightly against the base as a rope of hot jizz ejects out across me. It feels nice against my skin; playful almost.

The ghostly unicorn throws his head back and neighs, his abs held firm as several more pumps of cum eject from his shaft and splatter across my chin.

"Thank you." I tell him when the spunk finally stops falling.

The unicorn looks down at me with a look of satisfaction plastered across his face, then moments later evaporates into nothing.

"I hope you found what you were looking for." Melody tells me as I carry my bags out to the car.

I smile. "I did, actually."

The old woman is very pleased with this answer and, despite only knowing me for a day, gives me one final hug. "You're a very nice young man." She informs me.

"Thanks, Melody." I tell her.

"I hope that one day our paths will cross again." The old woman says as she releases her grip and I climb into the driver's seat of my car.

I look up at her. "Are you kidding me?" I'll be back within the week."

"Really?" Melody asks, her eyes lighting up.

"Just don't forget to put some more of that amazing soup on!"

As I drive away from the old manor I catch a glimpse of two ghostly unicorns standing off at the edge of a nearby field, patiently awaiting my return.

POUNDED BY THE GAY UNICORN FOOTBALL SQUAD

Throughout history, there will always be a select few who stand up against oppression, bigotry and intolerance. That is how it starts, with a handful of folks who just can't take it anymore and decide to do something about the position that they've been thrust into.

I've read about these people ever since I was a young man, but never in my wildest dreams did I ever think that I would grow up to be one.

When I first realized that I was gay, I wrongfully assumed that overcoming societies intolerance of my lifestyle would be my biggest hurdle. Of course, I had no way of knowing what would happen in the years to come.

As time passed the political climate changed greatly. People started to completely forget about borderlines of sexuality, instead turning their attention to the differences between humans and unicorns.

When I was younger, unicorns were the last thing anyone would have had a problem with, sweet horned beasts with beautiful flowing manes and killer style. But as unicorn music became more popular and began to invade the conservative homes of modern America, people started to take notice of this incoming foreign influence.

Soon enough, unicorn's turned from an edgy subculture to headline news.

After forming the UFL, unicorn football league, it was all over. The unicorns were faster than us, stronger than us, and better at interceptions. Unicorns had gone mainstream.

The craziest part, however, was when the unicorn lifestyle began to overshadow its human counterpart. Eventually, human football became a thing of the past as the unicorn games continued to produce more and more exciting matchups. A few of the players did manage to cross over and play in the UFL, but they remained closeted humans, never mentioning in any interviews that they were, in fact, not unicorns.

By the end of the transition, almost ninety percent of professional football players in American were out of a job.

Thankfully, I am one of the ten percent who remained, but it didn't come without a price. I may be openly gay, but the world at large can never know that I'm not actually a unicorn.

Keeping up appearances isn't as hard as you would think in the UFL. I basically just go about my day as any other player would; practicing all the time, doing endorsements, hanging out with the guys. Really, the only thing I have to worry about is that terrifying question that pops up every so often in interviews.

I remember the first time that it happened. My team, the Los Angeles Sparkles, had just won our second consecutive Hornbowl and we were all reeling from the victory. The press conference was uproarious and full of laugher, but everything got awkward quick when I took the microphone and was asked my first question of the night.

I vividly remember the little old woman standing up and adjusting the thick-rimmed glasses on her face as she glanced down at the notepad in her hand. "Aaron Duncan." She began. "Are you a unicorn?"

The question was so unexpected that I could barely function. My unicorn classification had never once been called into doubt, and why should it? I play just as hard out there on the field as the rest of my team. Not to mention the fact that there are plenty of other players in the UFL who seem much less like a unicorn than I do. Even *I* have my doubts.

I swallowed hard and tried my best to collect my thoughts. "Yes, I'm a unicorn. Why wouldn't I be?" I asked.

"Well, because you don't have a horn, or hooves!" Said the old woman, a sharp accusatory tone in her voice.

I laughed out loud, trying my best to put up a front. "I can assure you, I'm completely unicorn in every way. Next please."

A slew of hands all shot up, each of them with a much more pertinent question than whether or not I was a unicorn. I finished off the rest of the press conference well, but still, in the back of my mind, the woman's questions lingered. Was I really that obvious?

Over the offseason it was all that I could think about.

At first, I was angry that this woman would even ask such a thing. How dare she pry into my private life like that, as if it was any of her business what species I was. Officially, there is no rule stating that a human player cannot play in the UFL, and any aversion to such a thing was purely due to the fact that it had never been done before. Soon, my anger became directed towards myself, directed towards that fact that I didn't have the balls to stand up at the press conference and proudly say, "Yes, I am a human player in the unicorn football league."

It was at the moment that I realized what had to be done, and as the next year of football started I began asking around the team for their opinion of me coming out as a human player. Of course, all of the rest of the players had my back, including our unicorn coach.

The rest is all up to me.

Now standing behind the stage, I can barely stop shaking as I wait for the press wranglers to call me out onto the microphone. This is our first press conference of the season and everyone's in great spirits after winning our first game against the New England Rainbows. I should be thrilled right now, but I'm not. Only one thing is on my mind.

My friend and fellow player, Dirk Rando steps up behind me and puts a hoof on my shoulder. I turn around to face him, trying to hide the intense anxiety that seems to surge through every inch of my body.

"You're gonna be fine." Dirk says reassuringly. "Just remember that me and the rest of the guys have your back."

"I know." I tell him. "Thanks bud. It's just so crazy to think of how much this means to so many people, so many other's claiming unicorn but really just lonely, closeted humans."

"I'm not gonna pretend I know what it's like." Dirk tells me. "But I feel for you man, that's all I can say."

"I appreciate that." I tell him.

We both pause for a moment and in the silence I suddenly pick up on a strange electricity between us. I have always though of Dirk as one of my best friends, but in this moment of comfort I get the very distinct impression that something more is simmering just below the surface. This team means everything to me, Dirk included, but suddenly I'm understanding just how much their support and affection is actually worth. I've been so wrapped up in the question of whether or not I was a unicorn, that I forget what it meant to be human. How could I have been so blind to what was sitting right in front of me this whole time?

"Dirk." I suddenly say, my emotions overwhelming any semblance of rational thought. "I think I love…"

Suddenly, I hear my name being called from the stage and I straighten myself up, trying to smooth out any wrinkles on my suit.

"Go get 'em… human." Says dirk with a wink.

I smile, then turn around to head out onto stage and into a barrage of frantic flashbulbs. I give a confident wave and step up to the podium. "Hey everybody, thanks for coming out!"

The crowd settles down a bit as the first questioner stands up. I see her and my breath immediately catches in my throat, my heart skipping into double time. There before me is the same woman from last year's press conference, the little old lady who had first brought my human identity into question.

"Hello Aaron." The voice that haunts my dreams begins. "I don't know if you remember me. I was the woman who asked you last year about that allegations that you are actually secretly a human player in the Unicorn Football League."

"I remember." I tell her. "How could I forget?"

"I lot has happened since then." The woman continues. "Allegations continue to gain traction and several witnesses have come forward to report that you are, in fact, a human being. Now that all of this time has gone by, is there anything else you'd like to say about these accusations?"

The crowd goes quiet in anticipation of my response, which seems to be stuck somewhere deep down in the back of my throat. I so desperately want to reassure her that I am a unicorn, to lie through my teeth like I have a million times before and then get out of here as quickly as possible, but I just can't do it. I close my eyes and center myself, taking note of the way that the harsh lights of the room warm my skin. I take a deep breath.

"Yes." I finally respond. "There is something I'd like to say about that." I slowly look around the room at each and every one of the press agents, connecting with as many as I can. "I am a human being." I finally say. "Not a unicorn."

The entire crowd gasps audibly, and then frantically begins to shout

out questions for me to answer. I raise my hand up and quiet the mob.

"I'm a human and I'm proud to play in the Unicorn Football League." I say confidently. "I have the full support of my team and I look forward to continuing a great season with the Los Angeles Sparkles."

"Won't it be distracting to have a human player out on the field with all these unicorns?" Someone shouts.

I scoff. "Was it distracting before you knew I wasn't a unicorn? Of course not!"

"Why not just keep it to yourself?" Another one of the reporters asks.

"Because this is who I am." I retort. "I'm a human, I can't keep pretending to be a unicorn because that's what you all want from me. I'm not going to live a lie anymore."

I answer a few more queries and then eventually find myself dismissed when the question and answer time draws to a close.

Almost immediately, my phone starts buzzing with texts from friends and family. At first, I'm worried about what they might say, until I read a few of them and realize that there's nothing but love for me coming out of the unicorn closet. I scroll down the list of contacts voicing their support, smiling wide until I reach the first message. It's from Dirk.

"Hey man, come back to the locker room after the press conference." I read aloud. "Me and the guys want to talk to you about something."

I know full well that I have the team's support, but Dirk's words still put on me edge.

'On my way.' I text back, then head straight for the showers.

When I get there I find the whole team waiting for me, hanging out around the locker room and discussing something in a hushed tone.

"What's up guys?" I ask, letting the door swing shut behind me. I'm so nervous that literally I'm trembling.

Dirk stands and walks over to me, his brilliant ivory horn shining under the stark lighting from above. "Hey man, nice work out there." Dirk says.

A smile begins to creep across my face as the entire room full of unicorns begin neighing loudly and stomping their hooves.

"Thanks." I offer bashfully. "I appreciate it guys."

"You know, I was kinda suspicious for a while there, but I didn't want to say anything." The quarterback, Russell Marks tells me. "I guess I was right!"

I laugh. "What gave me away?"

Russell shrugs his unicorn shoulders. "I don't know, you don't really have a mane or anything."

I nod. He's right about that, and looking back I'm shocked that my bare neck never gave me away.

"Anyway." Dirk interjects. "Me and the guys were talking and..." He trails off.

"What is it?" I ask, equally confused and curious.

Dirk looks around at the rest of our teammates. "We're a really close team, you know?"

I nod.

"It's like... I think I love you, man." Dirk continues. "We all do."

Suddenly, my heart is flooded with emotion, all of these years anxiety and tension flowing out of me in a stream of salty tears. "I love you, too." I say. "All of you."

Dirk comes forward and nuzzles into me with his unicorn head, careful not to poke me with the point of his sharp horn. I wrap my arms around him and hold him close, enjoying the warmth of Dirk's warm fuzzy skin against mine.

Suddenly, it hits me. None of the guys are wearing their uniforms. In fact, none of the unicorns are wearing any clothes at all.

I step back in shock. "Whoa, what's going on here?" I stammer.

Dirk grins reassuringly. "Okay, don't freak out, but we've got something to ask you about."

Completely at a loss, I shake my head in exasperation and beg to know, "What is it?"

"Well, we were all talking, and a lot of us have never been with a human before. You know, slept with one." Says Dirk.

The second that my unicorn friend says this I can feel my cock start to harden within my pants.

"We were wondering if you'd be interested in showing us." Dirk asks.

"Showing you?" I question, knowing full well what he means but begging him to spell it out for me.

"Fucking us." Dirk clarifies.

My heart flutters and for a moment I feel as though I'm about to pass out right then and there. I had only just professed my undying love for these incredible beasts, and now they are trying to fuck me.

"Yes." I gasp, the words leaving my lips well before I have a chance to even consider the consequences. "Fuck me!" I say.

Slowly, I unbutton my shirt and reveal my toned chest and abs.

The unicorns begin to whinny happily, enjoying the show. I continue by slipping off my pants and then slowly, seductively removing my underwear until I am standing before them completely naked, my shaft rock hard and at the ready.

My teammates take me in with their huge unicorn eyes, enjoying the look of my muscular human body.

After a brief moment Dirk locks his gaze with mine, sharing a moment of unspoken affection, then he gracefully rolls over onto his back and opens his legs. The unicorn's massive cock is on display for me, a beautiful tower of sex just beaconing for my lips to be wrapped around it.

I know that my dynamic with the team will never ever be the same if I go through with this, but right now I'm too horny to even care, giving in to the animalistic side of my brain and letting my lust take the reigns. Seconds later, I'm on my knees letting this enormous hairy dick slide between my wet lips.

I bob up and down on the beast's rod for a while, letting him enjoy the sensation of my soft mouth across his hard, swollen unicorn cock. Dirk groans in a magical, beastly way, clearly enjoying himself as I pleasure him. I take his huge unicorn balls in my hand and cradle them as I service my teammate, barely noticing the other two beasts until they have clopped up on either side of me and turned themselves over, as well.

I reach out with both hands and take each of their cocks, pumping along with the rhythm of my mouth. All three of these MPV, Hornbowl winning unicorns begin to push back against me, thrusting their rods forward through the tightness of my firm grip.

I push down as far as I can on the cock in my mouth, choking a little and then relaxing enough to let it slide past my gag reflex. I hold his enormous shaft down there for a while, letting Dirk fully appreciate my sexual dexterity before coming back up for air.

I take in a huge gasp and then dive back down again, pushing even farther this time until my face is pressed hard against the unicorn's stomach. The beast puts its hooves behind my head and helps to keep me steady, holding me for as long as I can take it and then finally letting me up in a flurry of coughing sputters and teary eyes.

I glance around to see that there's an entire circle of unicorns lying on their backs around me now, their massive dicks standing straight up like giant goal posts towards the ceiling. Immediately, I begin to make my way around the circle, taking them three at a time before moving on to the next set.

The team enjoys me thoroughly, roughly making use of my human hands and lips. They pass me around with an animalistic power that should, honestly, be a little terrifying, but I can't help finding myself enjoying it.

My cock is swollen and hard from all this attention, and finally I just can't take it anymore. I sit up on all fours, letting the unicorns get a good look at my muscular, gay ass as I reach down and start to slowly stroke my dick. The team begins to neigh and stomp again, excited to have a chance at fucking me for real.

"You like that don't you?" I ask Dirk and the guys. I reach back with my hand and spread open my ass for them, egging them on. "You've probably been wondering all your life what it's like to fuck a real human dude, haven't you?"

I slip a single finger into my gay asshole, going deep and then pulling it out again.

Immediately, one of the unicorns, Tank the quarterback, clops over behind me and begins to mount. I look back over my shoulder at him, watching as the giant beast heaves himself over the back of my body and aligns his swollen cock with the entrance of my tight butthole.

"Fuck me!" I command.

"Hut, hut… Hike!" Tank says with a laugh. The unicorn quarterback thrusts forward and slides into my puckered asshole. I let out a long, gracious moan as he stretches me out, my tightness giving way to his enormous girth. The monster goes to work, slamming up into me as I brace myself against his powerful movements.

For never being with a human lover, Tank is incredibly adept at fucking me. The sensation is wonderful; a beautiful mixture of pleasure and fearful submission to this powerful, yet elegant, beast.

Before I know it, another one of the giant unicorns has climbed into position in front of me, his cock fat and swollen. I barely have time to open my mouth before he's thrusting his way inside, pushing deep down into my throat while I'm throttled from the back. The two unicorns instantly find a pulse between them as they slam me from both ends, rattling my large frame with every thrust while they gain speed inside of me. They go harder and harder, never letting up as I groan with pleasure between them until finally I'm worried I might actually get hurt.

Fortunately for me, this is precisely when the team decides to let two other unicorns have a go. The originals pull out of me and stomp away while two others quickly take their place, starting slow again and then building ferocity as they slam into me.

This pattern continues for a while until I lose track of how many giant unicorn cocks I've taken. It feels as though the entire team has had their way with my body, and even though the initial thought of being violated by so many beasts is disturbing, to say the least, there's no part of me that isn't completely satisfied and at ease. These aren't just any unicorns, these are the unicorns that I love.

Eventually, the team has had enough of this position and release me from their sexual unicorn-kabob. I wipe the tears from my eyes and the saliva from my mouth, and then look up at them, ready for more.

"I love you." I confess to Dirk as he stands in front of me. "I want us all to be together, the whole unicorn team."

"We want that, too." Dirk assures me. "We all want the same thing, and it's going to be beautiful."

One of the unicorns is lying on his back next to me now, and with all four of his hooves he seems to be motioning for me to climb onto him. An excited smirk crossing my face, I quickly crawl over to my teammate and straddle his huge, unicorn body, carefully lowering myself down so that his giant cock slides right up into my ass. I begin to ride him, enjoying myself immensely until I see another one of the beasts climbing into position behind us.

"Whoa buddy!" I say out loud, looking back at him as he heaves himself over the top of me. "I don't know about that."

No sooner have the words left my mouth does the beast behind me thrust himself firmly into my already taken asshole, successfully double penetrating me. I let out a yelp of surprise that slowly morphs into an animalistic growl as I find myself enjoying it. I push back towards them, slamming down hard against every upward thrust. Their members stretch me tight, filling me entirely as they throb together within my single hole.

It's not long before the unicorn football player behind me starts gaining speed, slamming harder and harder until the beast pushes deep within my asshole and spills out his hot load up my ass. The beast lets out a satisfied groan as he holds deep, filling me with pump after pump of sticky sperm and then, finally, pulling out so that another unicorn can have a chance within my aching human butthole.

Using the cum as lube, this new unicorn thrusts into me from behind and begins hammering away with equal fervor, steadily gaining speed like the last one until he explodes, as well. The unicorn player unleashes even more spunk inside of my asshole, mixing with the hot load that came before it. As he pulls out, some of the white liquid spills out of my tightness and runs down my toned legs in pearly streaks.

The unicorns continue to fuck me like this, taking turns within my asshole as the original beast pounds me from below. Eventually, there's no room left in my asshole for their magical unicorn cum, which overflows from my orifice every time that I'm unplugged.

I've taken about ten of their loads, with no end in sight. The entire team is here, waiting and ready to explode within me as an expression of our everlasting interspecies love.

"Cum inside me!" I scream at them. "Fucking cum inside my gay ass!"

I reach down and start to frantically beat my cock, pushing myself closer and closer to orgasm until finally I just can't take anymore and my body erupts with pleasure. The powerful sensation flows through me in waves, each one of them stronger than the next as I seize with ecstasy. I close my eyes and clench my teeth, barely able to stand the blissed out feelings that rock me from head to toe, while cum shoots from the end of my cock.

My screams of pleasure echo throughout the locker room and down the hallway, ricocheting off of the concrete walls.

When I've finally finished I find myself in a gay, fucked-silly daze, barely able to keep my eyes open as the beasts continue to ram me.

Finally, the last one in front finishes and the unicorn below pulls out of me, rolling me off of him and onto the locker room floor. I look up to see the final unicorn teammate standing over me and then smile happily as, moments later, he unleashes his unicorn load across my face.

I scan the eager crowd of reporters.

"Yes, you." I say with a smile, pointing to the little old woman in the front row of tonight's press conference. I remember a time when her face caused me more anxiety than I could bear, but by now I'd honestly consider her a friend.

The older woman stands and takes out her notepad as a few flashbulbs go off. "It's been quite the season for your team, completely undefeated going into the playoffs." She says. "That's a first in UFL history. To what do you owe your success this season?"

"Hard work." I tell her. "Determination... and love."

"There has been a lot happening off the field with the Los Angeles Sparkles, too." The woman says with a nod. "You came out as the leagues first openly human player, and then later when the entire team revealed that you were all participating in a massive, team wide romantic relationship with one another."

"That's correct." I tell her. "We play hard, and we love hard."

ABOUT THE AUTHOR

Dr. Chuck Tingle is an erotic author and Tae Kwon Do grandmaster (almost black belt) from Billings, Montana. After receiving his PhD at DeVry University in holistic massage, Chuck found himself fascinated by all things sensual, leading to his creation of the "tingler", a story so blissfully erotic that it cannot be experienced without eliciting a sharp tingle down the spine.

Chuck's hobbies include backpacking, checkers and sport.

Printed in Great Britain
by Amazon